HOLLY KELLER

I Am Angela

 Greenwillow Books, New York

For Ginny, Roger, Carl,
Amy, John, and Hector
with love

The preseparated two-color art was prepared with a pen-
and-ink line and halftone overlays done in pencil.
The text type is Kuenstler 480 Roman.

Library of Congress Cataloging-in-Publication Data
Keller, Holly.
I am Angela / by Holly Keller.
p.   cm.
Summary: Whether at camp, on a trip to the zoo,
walking a neighbor's dogs, or working on a class project,
Angela's love of nature is evident.
ISBN 0-688-14967-7
[1. Nature—Fiction.]   I. Title.
PZ7.K28132Iae   1997   [E]—dc20
96-5755   CIP   AC

CONTENTS

1. I Am Angela

Some things are really not fair, and having a birthday the day after Christmas is definitely one of them.

I am Angela, and my birthday is December 26. I can tell you that it always feels like a mistake.

My last birthday wasn't as bad as usual, although as usual nobody was exactly worked up about giving me more presents.

My brother, Ralph, who is very annoying most of the time, did a *great* magic show at my party, and Mama put pink roses on my cake. They were very good.

The year hasn't been exactly what I would call the best, but I'm finally old enough to go to sleep-away camp.

The pictures of the camp look pretty nice, especially the one where a girl is reading up in a tree. There's another good picture of kids catching toads.

You can't count on too much from the pictures, though. Sometimes things just don't work out the way they're supposed to. But then, of course, sometimes they do.

2.

An Amazing Whistle

I'm in cabin 6 at Camp Wabonka-in-the-Hills. The summer has gone by really fast, and it wasn't too bad.

I have all my important things with me, like my bird book and the butterfly net Ralph said I could take if I guarded it with my life, which I do—most of the time.

My insect collection is temporarily living in a mayonnaise jar because Cynthia, who sleeps in the bed next to mine, says just looking at it gives her the creeps. Luckily the jar fits into my cubby, where she can't see it.

My counselor's name is Midge, and she's nice. This morning we had a choice of basketball or a nature walk. I went on the nature walk, and as usual I was the only one from cabin 6.

I found a very cool lizard. I brought it back to the cabin after dinner, but I wouldn't say that everyone loved it.

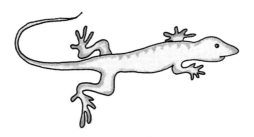

Cynthia wanted to know what was on my head, so I explained how the nature group made hats from skunk cabbage leaves. She said it smelled hideous. I put

the lizard and the hat outside on the porch and read my bird book until rest period was over.

This afternoon's activity was softball. It was the last game of the summer.

I started hating softball about the third day of camp, when the teams got picked. Midge woke us up early that morning and told us to meet cabins 5 and 7 on the field for practice right after breakfast.

I wasn't in any big hurry to get there because I didn't think I was going to be very good at it. Cynthia said it was easy and I shouldn't worry, but I'm not exactly the sportsy type. Besides, things like softball always look easy when other people do them.

The practice was terrible. Every girl was supposed to go up to home plate and hit

some balls. When the batter hit three good balls in a row, Midge said, "Good job," and the girl went into the outfield to practice catching. Nothing to it. Of course the first time *I* tried to hit the ball, the bat slipped out of my hand and skittered halfway to third base.

I heard Cynthia giggle, and I know my face got blotchy because it always does when I'm nervous.

Midge said I could keep trying, but I really didn't see the point. Finally she gave me a glove and told me to go way out into the outfield and catch anything that came my way.

I can tell you that the only thing that came out there was a bunch of butterflies, so I picked some daisies from a clump the lawn mower had missed.

It took forever to set up the teams. Each captain chose twelve girls: nine regulars and three backups. I got picked to be the third backup on the red team (big surprise), and after that everybody pretty much ignored me, which was just fine with me.

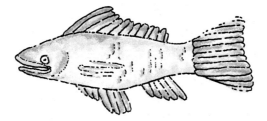

Sometimes when the other girls go to softball, I can convince Midge to let me go to the nature cabin. I made some excellent fish prints the other day. The bass came out the best.

I also made a little house for Simon, the box turtle I found on the road. It fitted right into the corner of the shower stall and was of course in nobody's way, but Helen made a big stink about it. She uses so much shampoo, it probably would have killed Simon anyway.

The wildflowers at camp are very beautiful, and Midge said it is okay to pick some specimens from time to time. I keep them in old cans around the cabin. Samantha is allergic to quite a lot of things, though, so often I have to throw most of them out pretty quickly.

Last weekend Midge said I had to go to the lower-camp relay races even if I didn't want to. She said there wouldn't be enough girls on our cabin's team otherwise.

In the middle of the sack race Roberta in cabin 7 caught a giant bullfrog and was holding it upside down by the legs.

I was really mad. I pulled my sack off and marched over to the girl and asked her how *she* would like to be hanging upside down by her legs.

Our team was disqualified from the race,

and Midge was furious. She told me that now I *had* to go to arts and crafts, and that's when the good news started to happen.

The arts and crafts tent is in the middle of a grove of pine trees. No matter how hot it is everywhere else, it always feels cool there. It's one of my favorite places.

Anyway, that day I met a girl there named Alice, who was missing her two front teeth. She told me she had lost them when she fell off her bicycle, and it made

my teeth hurt just to hear about it. But then she told me that the good thing was that now she could whistle. She showed me how she put her fingers in her mouth, pressed down, and blew. It was very impressive.

I thought about that whistle on my way back to cabin 6 and decided to give it a try. Naturally I wasn't going to knock my teeth out or anything like that, but I just wanted to see if it would work.

I put my fingers in my mouth just the way Alice had, pressed down, and blew as hard as I could. You wouldn't have believed the sound I made. Even I didn't believe it. It was nothing like Alice's little whistle.

So I started practicing every chance I got—that is, whenever I was sure nobody else could hear me.

I gave Alice a demonstration a few days later, and she said it was "amazing," which I guess it was. I made her promise not to tell anyone.

Then one very hot afternoon last week when I *had* to go to softball, I was sitting on the bench with all my fingers and toes crossed, hoping I wouldn't have to play.

The blue team was winning 10 to 2 in the last inning, and nobody was very interested. When Samantha finally hit a

ball all the way into the outfield, Midge was about the only one who cheered.

I don't know why I decided to do it right at that minute, but before I knew it, I stood up on the bench, put my fingers into my mouth, pressed down, and blew. The sound was so astounding that the pitcher covered her ears.

"Go, Red!" I yelled. "Score that run!"

Everybody stood perfectly still and looked at me. So I just whistled again.

Suddenly the whole red team was on its feet, stamping and cheering. Samantha ran around the bases and made it all the way to third.

When the next batter was up, I waited to see what would happen. The pitch was good, the hit was solid, and I let out another big whistle.

It was pretty funny. The team just went crazy. Samantha made it home and scored another run. Midge said I was the best cheerleader ever.

The game this afternoon was for the championship. A lot of people came to hear me whistle, and the girls on the red team decorated their hats with leaves and flowers. I know it was supposed to be for me, but they looked pretty silly.

I had a special box to stand on right out in front that said "Cheerleader" on it in big red letters. *That* I liked! Of course now the team had to play with only two backups, but I seriously doubt that anyone cared.

All I had to do was whistle every time someone got a good hit or scored a run. The team did all the rest.

The blue-team captain said she didn't think it was fair, but sour grapes are never big attention getters.

The final campfire was right after the game. I won the nature prize, which is a pair of slippers that look like spiders, and they are G-R-E-A-T. I think I'll put them on and whistle one more time.

3.
Buddies

The easiest way to know if the sandwich in your lunch bag is tuna fish is to smell it. Which is exactly what I always do before putting my lunch in my backpack.

Once, before I started checking my lunch, a tuna fish sandwich made my gym shorts smell like Ralph's turtle tank when he doesn't clean it for a month.

So the day Scout Troop 629, of which I

am a member, went to the zoo, the first thing I did was smell my lunch.

"It's cream cheese and jelly," Mama called from the kitchen, because she knew.

I put my lunch and my bird book into my backpack and went outside to watch for Ms. Hapgood's van.

When we got to the zoo, Ms. Hapgood had us all line up alongside the van so she could tell us about the buddy system, which she does every time we go on a trip.

Kathleen and I are always buddies, so we know this routine pretty well. The minute

Ms. Hapgood calls, "Buddies," we're supposed to drop everything, find our buddy, and hold up our hands. But Ms. Hapgood never understands that just because you *know* something doesn't mean you can always do it.

About five minutes after we left the parking lot, she decided to do a practice.

I heard her call, "Buddies," but a squirrel was just about to take a peanut out of my hand, and I didn't want to scare him away. Anyhow, I knew it was just a practice run.

Kathleen said, "Angela's missing already," and Ms. Hapgood went ballistic. I think that's when the day started to go wrong.

It was feeding time when we got to the monkey house. The place was packed, and it was raaa-ther hot and smelly.

A baby monkey was making a big racket
because the piece of orange that he was
eating fell out of his hand and landed
outside the cage. I watched him try to
reach it by sticking his hand through the
bars, but he just couldn't stretch far
enough. It made me feel sad.

When the guard walked away, I picked up the orange, and without really thinking about it, I whispered to the monkey that I was going to give it back. Of course it was just my luck that at that very minute another guard saw me and blew his whistle.

The next thing I heard was Ms. Hapgood asking, "Where is Angela?" which made me mad, and then Frieda giggled and said, "She's talking to a monkey," and that made me furious. Then right away Ms. Hapgood yelled, "Buddies," and that was the end of that. Everybody was pretty anxious to get out of there anyway.

Ms. Hapgood said we would spend about fifteen minutes at the exhibit of nocturnal animals and then have lunch. Big cheer for that.

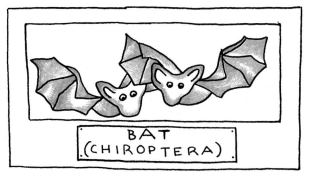

BAT
(CHIROPTERA)

It was really spooky inside the nocturnal animals' building, but the bats were amazing. I tried to get Elizabeth to wait until her eyes adjusted so she could see how cool they were, but she wasn't too excited.

I don't know exactly how it happened, but somehow I forgot about the time and the troop.

I was looking at the raccoons when I realized that none of the other Scouts was anywhere around. I followed the arrows to

the exit, but there weren't any Scouts outside either. Wouldn't you just know that the one time Ms. Hapgood should have done a buddy check, she forgot?

I knew that everyone else was having lunch, so I guessed I should, too. I sat down on a bench and took a few bites of my sandwich.

Nobody seemed to be looking for me, and I felt a little weird sitting there all by myself, so I decided to go to the bird house, which was next door.

There were birds flying around all over the place. I actually found three of the finches that are in my bird book.

You have to go up and down quite a lot of ramps to get from one end of the bird house to the other, and when I finally went through the door that said "out," I had no idea where I was.

Later Judith told me that when the troop got to the picnic ground and everyone had unpacked her lunch, Ms. Hapgood did a buddy check and guess who was missing?

Kathleen said that she'd kept hoping I would show up, and that when I didn't, she was pretty worried. It was nice to hear, because at first everyone else was just mad. I guess Ms. Hapgood went a little crazy and made everybody pack up her lunch one, two, three.

Phoebe said they had to run through the reptile house at about one hundred miles an hour and they couldn't stop to look at anything. Claire got a cramp, and Suzanne told me that Robin said something about my being eaten by a poisonous snake. Very nice.

Well, I guess they had to zip through the big-cat house, too, and when Kathleen complained about not being able to see the lions, Ms. Hapgood started screaming at everybody.

It was pretty hard not to laugh, though, when Amanda told me how Ms. Hapgood made them look under all the doors in the bathroom.

But I think things got really out of control when Frieda decided that I might have been kidnapped and she started to cry. Have you ever noticed that crying is a little bit like yawning—you know, when one person does it, everybody else does it, too?

That's what happened, and Ms. Hapgood decided to call in the police. Luckily the troop had to pass the animal rides to get to the police station, because that's where I was.

After I left the bird house, I wandered around for a little while until even I had to admit that I was probably hopelessly lost. I really *was* just about to tell a guard when I found the animal rides.

I didn't think things would be any worse if I stopped to watch for a few minutes, and that's when I met Mr. Curtis.

There were only a few kids riding animals that afternoon, so Mr. Curtis noticed me standing there by myself right away. I told him what had happened, and he agreed that I should tell a guard about being lost. But he said I could have a quick

ride on the camel first if I wanted to. And of course I did.

So there I was, sitting high up on the camel saddle being an Egyptian princess, when I saw Ms. Hapgood and the troop zooming along with nearly everybody crying.

I started waving both hands, and when they didn't notice that, I decided to try a whistle. I did the usual thing—put my fingers in my mouth, pressed down, and blew—and got the usual result. Even the camel stopped in its tracks.

Claire saw me first and started shouting right away about not getting to see *anything,* and Phoebe said that they had had a terrible day and that it was, as usual, my fault.

You might have thought that at least Ms. Hapgood would have been glad to see me, but instead she came marching over and in a very strange voice said, "Angela, please get down this minute. We have been looking for you for over an hour."

The day could have really ended up a mess, but Mr. Curtis saved it. After Ms.

Hapgood had calmed down a little, he came over to the group and introduced himself. He said he thought it would be very nice to celebrate finding me by giving everyone in the troop a ride on one of the animals.

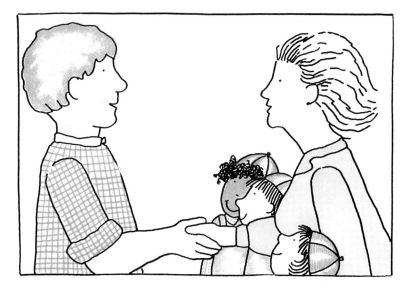

Naturally it took about two seconds for them all to stop being angry and decide that they were really glad that I was okay.

Mr. Curtis gave me a little wink and offered Ms. Hapgood a ride in the donkey cart, but she said she was pretty tired and would rather sit on a bench.

So Amanda and Claire rode on the camels, and Kathleen, Frieda, and Suzanne rode on the elephant. Phoebe, Judith, and Robin each got a pony. We all had a great time, although we didn't all admit it. . . .

When we got back to the van, Ms. Hapgood decided to have a last buddy check. Everybody found her partner and yelled, *"Buddies,"* and this time I was definitely not missing.

At dinnertime Ralph wanted to know how I liked the zoo. I said it was good. Very good.

4.

A Winter Walk

It's very hard to buy surprise Christmas presents when you never have enough money and usually have to end up borrowing it from the person who's getting the present. I started worrying about that right after Thanksgiving.

Our upstairs neighbor's name is Mr. Murdock, and he has four dogs. He walks them around the block every afternoon, and you can tell that he's not too happy about it.

So one day when I saw him outside, I asked him if he'd like to hire me to walk his dogs for him until Christmas. I pointed out that it would save him a lot of time and it wouldn't even be that expensive.

He wasn't too interested at first, but after I came up with about twenty more advantages, he finally said okay.

Mr. Murdock offered to pay me two dollars a day, and I figured that would make me the richest person I knew and definitely solve the Christmas present problem.

Mr. Murdock's poodle's name is Deirdre, and she has one of those weird poodle haircuts. Buster is a dachshund who refuses to go out unless he's wearing his sweater. Spud is a dalmatian, and he won't walk next to Deirdre, which I can totally understand, and Hector, the terrier, never wants to go out at all. I think it's because he's afraid someone will take his food away while he's gone. The minute he sees the leash, he runs to his food dish and growls.

So getting ready to go out takes longer than you would believe. First I have to stuff Buster into his sweater, because the sweater is a turtleneck and Buster has no neck. Then I have to bribe Hector with a biscuit so he'll stop growling long enough for me to put on his leash. Deirdre runs to the door, and Spud runs into the bathroom. On the first day I was already thinking that two dollars a day was not enough.

Going down the stairs with four dogs isn't too much fun either. Spud and Deirdre have long legs, and they run down the stairs about three steps at a time. Buster has such short legs that he's still up at the top when the other two are almost at the bottom. Hector just refuses to move.

The first day of my job we all came crashing out the door onto the street and almost knocked Ms. Bidwell and her two bags of groceries into the garbage can. It wasn't exactly a cool start.

When we actually got to the walking part, I kept Spud and Buster on one side and Deirdre and Hector on the other. This worked pretty well until Buster decided to go after a squirrel and Deirdre attacked the mail carrier.

I more or less got things under control by the time we reached the first corner, but that was definitely no thanks to Hector.

Hector goes totally ballistic every time he sees food, and you have no idea how much food there is on an ordinary street until you walk with Hector. By the time we went around the whole block, we probably passed three or four restaurants, a bagel place, a grocery, and a delicatessen, and

Hector had to stop, sniff, and growl at every one.

Buster tried to get Hector to move by barking nonstop, and Deirdre lay down on the street and looked bored. Spud just kept walking until his leash was pulled so tight he'd probably have flown to the moon if I'd let go, which I actually considered doing.

This was all pretty annoying, especially since it kept happening every day.

At the end of the week Mr. Murdock gave me fourteen dollars and told me I was doing a really great job. I tried to think about all the Christmas presents I was going to buy.

The second week wasn't too bad, and we were halfway through the third, which I'm happy to say was also the last, when it started to snow.

Everybody was really excited about having a white Christmas except Deirdre, who didn't like getting her feet wet. You wouldn't believe how a walk around the block can feel like a ten-mile hike if you have a dog who stops every three minutes to shake the snow off her feet.

On Thursday afternoon Ms. Henley came along pulling her little boy, Reggie, on a sled. The problem was that Reggie was eating a cookie, and he was very close to Hector.

Ms. Henley is very friendly and she stopped to say hello and ask me about school and how my mother was and how Ralph was, and naturally that was when Hector made his move.

All of a sudden Reggie started to shriek, and Hector bolted with Reggie's cookie in his mouth. Buster and Deirdre took off after him, and Spud ran after Deirdre.

Of course dumb Ralph had to look out the window just at that minute, and when he saw me being pulled along, he started shouting, "Mush, huskies, mush," which I'm sure he thought was very funny.

All I could think of was what Mr. Murdock would say if one of his dogs got away.

We actually ran all around the block, and when we came around the last corner, Ms. Henley and Reggie were still there. Luckily Deirdre suddenly remembered that she had snow on her feet and came to a sliding

stop. Hector, Buster, and Spud fell all over one another in a heap, but when Reggie saw Hector, he started to shriek again.

I more or less shoved the dogs into the house and dragged them upstairs.

Mr. Murdock was waiting for us at the door. I guess he didn't notice that we were all covered with snow and that the dogs were in a terrible tangle, because he said he thought I was an excellent dog walker and asked me if I would like to have the job on a permanent basis. Right.

So I crossed about every finger and toe that would cross and told him that I liked his dogs a lot, but that I was really mostly a bird and insect person and I was about ready to stop and buy my Christmas presents.

I bought a lot of very cool things for

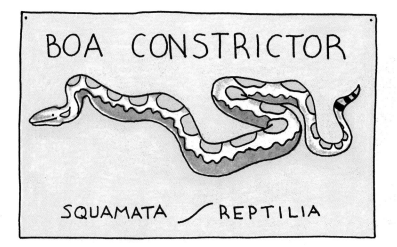

BOA CONSTRICTOR

SQUAMATA / REPTILIA

everyone, including an excellent snake poster for Ralph, although I don't know why.

But guess who got the best present of anybody? I did.

I suppose Mr. Murdock didn't believe that I was *just* a bird and insect person because the day after Christmas he brought me a puppy he got from the pound. He said he thought I might like walking just one dog instead of four, and someone had told him that it was my birthday.

Gus is tan and white and has a very bushy tail, and we are together all the time.

This was probably my best Christmas and birthday ever.

5.
Spring Is in the Air

Some mornings I think I should just turn off the alarm and go back to sleep until the next day. One of those mornings happened a few weeks ago, but I didn't know it until it was too late.

The alarm rang, and Harriet, my parakeet, started squawking "yoo-hoo, yoo-hoo" until I couldn't stand it anymore. (Ralph and his friend Izzy taught her how to do that—ha-ha.) Once I got up to put the cover on her cage, the day just automatically got started.

One of my spider slippers was snagged by the vacuum recently, and two of its legs came off. It makes me feel terrible every time I put it on. So there I was with another irritating thing, and I hadn't even gotten to the bathroom yet.

Naturally, I wasn't too happy to find Ralph already in the kitchen having his breakfast when I went in to check my flower pots. I'd sent away for some Venus flytrap seeds, and I followed the planting directions exactly, but so far nothing had happened.

"Stuff like that never grows," Ralph said, because no day can get started without his two cents.

When I told him that when these did, he would be their first meal, he stood up on the chair and announced, "Beware, beware. Here comes Angela and her army of carnivorous plants!"

Don't I wish.

In school that morning Mr. Stitch said he thought it would be nice to make an exhibit of everything we could think of that happened in the spring. He asked who would like to be in charge of setting it up.

I said I would, because it didn't sound too bad. Which just goes to show how wrong a person can be.

The next day James and Fred brought in a box of old baseball cards. Sam brought some flower seeds that were left over from last year, and Amanda brought a box of Kleenex. She has terrible allergies, so all she thinks about in the spring is her nose.

I brought some tulip bulbs and a jar of tadpoles from the pond near school. Mr. Stitch gave a long speech about cruelty to animals, because he was sure the tadpoles would die, and I had to promise that I would take them back to the pond. So there went the only interesting thing in the whole stupid exhibit.

Kathleen found a robin's egg that had fallen out of a nest somewhere, and she put it on the table, but I can tell you that nobody was running to see *that* exhibit.

Things actually began looking up the next day sort of unexpectedly. Ralph and I found a cocoon on a branch in the park. Ralph broke the whole branch off the bush, and I brought it into school for the exhibit.

I told everybody to stand by because something very surprising was going to come out. I didn't need Ralph to tell me how stupid *that* was, but I had to do something.

James started asking about every half hour when it was going to hatch, and

Amanda decided it was her job to announce every morning that nothing had hatched.

Things were getting so bad that I started to feel a sore throat coming on that would keep me home in bed for quite a while. Luckily the weekend came first.

When I got to school on Monday, there was a whole crowd outside my classroom door. Mr. Stitch was in the middle of it. His face was bright red, and he was waving his arms around like a windmill.

I heard somebody say, "There she is," and the next thing I knew they were all around me like those gnats you run into in the summer, and everyone was talking at once. So I figured that something had finally happened with the cocoon.

I opened the classroom door just a crack, but I couldn't really see anything. Then about a hundred people started to shout, "Go in, go in," all at once, so I did.

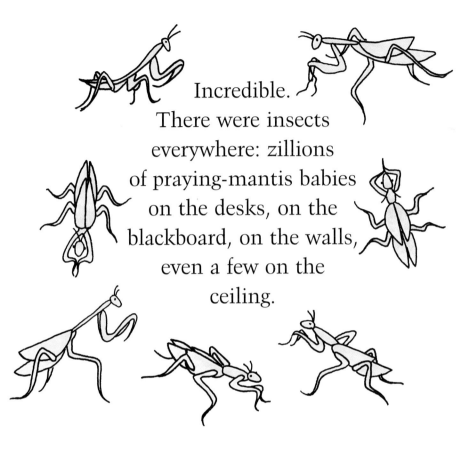

Incredible.
There were insects
everywhere: zillions
of praying-mantis babies
on the desks, on the
blackboard, on the walls,
even a few on the
ceiling.

I caught one and brought it into the hall.
I opened my hands just a crack to show Mr.
Stitch what it looked like, and naturally the
thing jumped out and landed on his sleeve.

Everyone started shrieking, and Mr. Stitch was totally out of control. Ralph said they could hear the noise all the way up in the sixth grade.

I told Mr. Stitch that we could catch them if he would let me take some kids back into the room. That's when bigger trouble started, because everybody wanted to help.

Finally Mr. Stitch picked ten kids, and we went back in.

Claire pulled up the window shades so we could see better, and it was really funny. Peter found a praying mantis on his lunch box, and Fred found one on Mr. Stitch's hat. (We all agreed not to share that piece of information.) There were so many of them

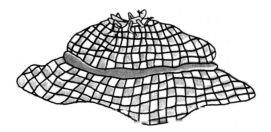

it took us almost two hours to get them into Claire's gym bag and the four or five lunch boxes we'd emptied out.

We took the praying mantises into the yard to let them go, and everyone in the second grade came to watch. It was very cool. All the praying-mantis babies marched off into the grass together.

Mr. Stitch had a terrible headache and had to go home. We had a substitute teacher for the rest of the day, and I don't think that anyone was too unhappy about that—especially me.

It isn't exactly true that we let *all* the praying mantises go, because I kept two in my snack bag. I definitely wanted to show them to smarty-pants Ralph. Even he had to admit that they were impressive.

And something else happened that he had to admit he was wrong about: My Venus flytraps started growing.

I put the two praying mantises into an old fish tank with some grass and branches and covered it with a piece of cardboard. Ralph made some airholes in the cardboard, and that was pretty nice of him. He even helped me carry the tank to school the next day, along with the Venus-flytrap seedlings.

But the best thing was that Mr. Stitch, who I guess was feeling better, made a sign for the exhibit table.

ANGELA'S WONDERFUL
SPRINGTIME SHOW

When he tacked it on the wall, everybody clapped. I don't think the class will forget *that* exhibit for a long time! I know I won't.

It's almost summer again, and I decided to write to my counselor, Midge, at Camp Wabonka-in-the-Hills. I told her about the spring exhibit and how excited I was to be coming back to camp. I drew a picture of a big praying mantis on the envelope. I hope she likes it.

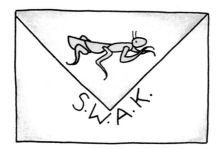